To the children
Boys and Girls
Enjoy this interesting
novel!

Sincerely
Marlene Mawson Sabeh

A Little Odd

by Marlene Mansour Sabeh

Bloomington, IN Milton Keynes, UK

AuthorHouse™
1663 Liberty Drive, Suite 200
Bloomington, IN 47403
www.authorhouse.com
Phone: 1-800-839-8640

AuthorHouse™ *UK Ltd.*
500 Avebury Boulevard
Central Milton Keynes, MK9 2BE
www.authorhouse.co.uk
Phone: 08001974150

This book is a work of fiction. People, places, events, and situations are the product of the author's imagination. Any resemblance to actual persons, living or dead, or historical events, is purely coincidental.

© 2006 Marlene Mansour Sabeh. All rights reserved.

No part of this book may be reproduced, stored in a retrieval system, or transmitted by any means without the written permission of the author.

First published by AuthorHouse 3/14/2006

ISBN: 1-4208-6229-4 (sc)

Printed in the United States of America
Bloomington, Indiana

This book is printed on acid-free paper.

To every boy or girl who, at times, finds it thorny to adjust in this overwhelmingly complex world.

To Lebanon for empowering me with a dream and to America for allowing me to fulfill it.

Also, to my heart and soul, Abraham and Meera.

Acknowlegements

I start at the source. My thanks to my omnipresent almighty God, my wonderful parents who taught me about accepting fate: My mother for guiding me through the –not always glamorous- years and my late father whose kind and generous soul carved my existence forever. To my Marissa who redefined the word sister in silent sacrifices and perpetual selflessness, my brother Maher for the precious unforgettable childhood years, my son Abraham whose goodness melts my heart away, my little princess Meera who teaches me a lesson of endurance everyday, my amazing friends: Zeina for her relentless love of life and Hanan for always believing in me, and last but not least my ultimate thanks to my best friend, the shoulder I cry on (very often), my rock, my companion, the father of my children, my husband and soul mate for his unconditional love, innate class, remarkable sense of humor and undying support.

I am forever thankful to all my Lebanese and American genuine friends who touched me with their kindness and unquestionable love. I am nothing without all of them.

Chapter One

They didn't listen to me. I cried, I screamed, I pouted and I shouted but they didn't listen to me. I stayed in my room for a whole week, had all my meals in there, hoping they would change their minds but they didn't. Their decision was made. And it was final. I slowly realized that my rebellion was facing a dead end. I surrendered. Slowly, sadly.

I was yet to embark on a quaint journey, facing the unknown and embracing a new life.

How can we leave our country, our home, our land? and why? They told me that the war had started to affect the economy and ultimately our life. "So what?" I thought. I was born here, I belonged here. We belonged here; but they didn't listen to me. "Dad, things will eventually pick up. The antebellum era will be back...You will see. We have to be patient "I had said to my father. "Ramsey, You are thirteen, you are young. You will adjust so easily in America and we will have, as a family, a better opportunity to improve our life and fulfill our dreams. You and your sister will be happy,

I promise." My father answered somberly. How would I adjust? I don't want to adjust. I want to stay. I want to stay. I want to stay. I thought.

Lebanon is a beautiful small country situated in the Middle East region of the globe. Its 10452 Km^2 sprawled along a coastal line on the Mediterranean sea. The uniqueness of its location earned it an attractive aspect and subjected it to a long painful war struggle, in order to rule it and exploit its strategic spot.

The major civil war had broken out in 1975 and lasted for twenty years which damaged the financial structure of the country over that period. Almost every family was affected by the war. Beside the long periods of bombing, the loss of jobs and closing of businesses impaired the prosperous life that Lebanese people led prior to the devastating war. It was a bitter reality for the people to face and cope with as reasonably as they could. Many of them however sought a better chance for living in different countries. Many Western and European governments opened the door to immigrants coming from the region.

My parents had been putting this idea off for over a year but my father's catering business was suffering severely and times were getting bad for all of us.

My uncle George has been living in the United States of America in a small town called "Fall River" in the state of Massachusetts for over twenty years. After many attempts, he finally succeeded at convincing my parents to emigrate to the USA. It was a hard, long contemplated, solemn decision. The one you probably make only once in your life and upon which, lies destiny, future and wishfully happiness.

The decision was final. Only deep in my heart, the hope of one day, going back "home" soothed my troubled thoughts and pacified my brewing hostility.

"Welcome to America!" the immigration officer greeted us.

The broad smile on his tanned pleasant face reminded me of my uncle Steve who cried his heart out as he waved goodbye at Beirut's airport. It didn't matter anymore who cried and who held his tears. We are here. Now. We are in America.

Logan airport in Boston welcomed us like it does millions of people, with pale walls, dark floors and constant uninterrupted noise. My father, my mother, my sister Raya and I headed towards the exit door pushing our eight suitcases, passports in hands, sadness in heavy hearts and hopes up in the sky.

Like most evenings in Boston's Januaries, the cold wind entered the lungs crisp and fierce. "It is too cold!" I said, looking at my parents and Raya. Shaking, exhausted and speechless, they stood on the curb, lost in a sea of hazy thoughts and Boston's evening lights. Comfortable in the cozy and warm taxi, we embarked on an hour and a half ride from the airport to Fall River, towards Southern Massachusetts.

The sun had set by then and the glimmering lights of downtown Boston dazzled our eyes. "Fasten your seat belts, please" interrupted the cab driver. Seat belts! We never worried about them in Lebanon. "I don't like this tight belt around my waist" I thought. I felt trapped, almost suffocating from the nostalgic anticipation, the perplexing fear and the overwhelming sense of misery.

Chapter Two

"How are you, son?" My uncle George uttered in a loud emotional voice as he gave me a long tight hug. "I'm fine uncle George, How are YOU?" I answered. "Oh! happy to see all of you. I was looking forward to your safe arrival." He said. Uncle George then hugged my father. The two brothers hadn't seen each other for a very long time and their loving reunion brought tears to everybody's eyes.

"This is the most suitable apartment I could find. You know, I was looking for one that is close to my house!" He bragged, winking at my father. I looked around the rather tiny space where we were standing. Our suitcases, crumbled on the wall-to-wall carpeted floor held all our belongings, our personal items, our memories. The dark paneling of all the walls paralleled the gloomy emptiness inside my soul. Vivid Flashes of our spacious bright house in Beirut, accented by the vast lively garden that my mother kept impeccably blooming put this lousy apartment to shame in no time. I walked toward the kitchen and the fact that there was no separating wall between it and the living room immediately struck me. "It is all hardwood floors underneath!", announced uncle George with pride. "Wood?" I exclaimed. "All houses are made out of wood here, Ramsey" My father interjected. "Does my room have a balcony?" I said as I walked in one of the rooms adjacent to the living room. "Balcony?? This apartment, along with almost all others in this country do not have balconies, son. The harsh winters are long and cold. Besides, people prefer porches; porches as in houses, of course. Anyway, there is a very cozy yard in the back of the building where you can play with your sister and friends, come the summer" answered uncle George. I looked at my mother who was explicably worn out from the exhausting flight and I saw streaks of hollowness in her eyes. She must be wondering how tough it would be to adapt to almost everything new and how long will it take her and us to be able to feel safe and happy. She might already miss her lifelong friend and neighbor Samia who, back at Beirut airport, made a vow to my mom that she will never have espresso coffee until she comes back from America.

Jet lag was a seven hours difference between the two countries which messed up our sleeping pattern for a whole week. It wasn't enough that we felt edgy all day, we had the sleepless white nights to deal with. The emptiness, the homesickness and the loneliness were too hard to deal with. We hardly communicated regarding our feelings. We needed to be practical. Talking about emotions was too delicate, too steep of a platform. We each withdrew in our own deep souls, tackling what's left of the past and praying for a better tomorrow. The Today we were living was engulfed in a sea of questions, vague perspectives and denied emotions.

Fall River did all its best to make us feel home and content. Its streets, unlike the nonsymmetrical routes in Lebanon, were aligned in perfect peaceful harmony, offering the feeling of recognizable ease. In the inner city, mostly towards the East and South, most houses are multi-family having the same English basic structure and architecture. In the North of the city, dispersed are the single family upper grade houses. This is where the most prominent families of Fall River resided. Well manicured lawns, above ground swimming pools, sunrooms and gazebos were present in almost all the houses in that section of the city. It gave Fall River an upper class flavor with respect to its adjacent cities.

Several decades ago, Fall River was living its glorious days. The numerous amount of Mills and factories gave it the reputation and prosperity that was long envied for. If you walk down by the Flint area, you can still see the old deserted huge buildings that witnessed the success and booming of those days. Some minor factories are still in business until our actual day, but their output is minimal compared to the old times.

The population of the city consisted of a diversity of old and new comers from all over the countries and regions of the world. However, the largest community that lived in Fall River is mostly Portuguese. Immigrants from Portugal started flowing in to New England in general since the nineteen fifties. It was a major attraction to them mainly because of its location on the coast of the Atlantic facing Europe. As soon as they settled down, Portuguese immigrants assimilated as fast as they could and adjusted and started working, going to school and building families and legacies of their own. Now, they have become a major part of the Fall River society and have contributed in the progress of labor and education.

Despite the many similarities between Portuguese and Lebanese traditions, mostly due to the reign of the Arabic empire in Portugal for a long time in the past, we still didn't have a lot in common. For example, the language which we all agreed on the fact that it was hard to learn. We were trying so hard to fit in, to find a window to reach out and belong in any way. Many of my uncle's friends kept telling us it was too early, that we needed to give it time, time... It's all we have. My mother was turning into an incredibly quiet person, trying to absorb all our points of views, all our complaints and our search for a new identity. My father was spending countless hours with uncle George looking for a job, any job.

Success came at last! He got a job at a gas station filling gas 12 hours a day. We didn't say anything to each other that day. It was too inexplicable. We kept looking at each other, each trying to assess the new situation according to his/her standards. At least, he would be doing something. Anything. Instead of staying home, feeling homesick, missing his friends, coworkers and land. It was, in a way, the first step for our family towards living the American dream. Isn't it why we left everything behind and came here?

The struggle was in no way diminishing nor waning. There will be days filled with foggy sadness, irreversible regrets and placid despair. In no easy mean, America will be our second "Home". It was a long rocky, dejecting road.

Chapter Three

Uncle George enrolled me in Talbot Middle school located on Melrose Street. On my first day of school, uncle George picked me up early at seven in the morning. He offered to take me to school because my father was already working since five that morning and couldn't take off. Flocks of students were pouring in the middle section of the school grounds, either from school buses or from parents cars.

Nobody looked at me. Nobody knew me. I knew nobody. We had to sign in the main office, before heading upstairs to meet with my guidance counselor. A guidance counselor! I never had one. Why do I need one? What am I supposed to tell this guy?

As soon as my uncle recognized my counselor's name on the third door down the hallway, he stopped and looked at me and smiled "That's him, Ramsey. Mr. Perry". I cleared my throat and said: "Ok." Uncle George knocked at the door and almost immediately, an assertive voice from behind the dark wooden door invited us in "Come in." I grabbed the door knob and opened the door to see a rather middle aged man sitting behind a large dark desk, intensively working on his computer. He looked up, smiled and said: "well, hello there". Uncle George was quick to answer and introduce us to my guidance counselor: "Mr. Perry, this is my nephew Ramsey Remy. we talked on the phone yesterday. I" Mr. Perry interrupted: "Oh Yes! Mr. Remy. This is your brother's son who recently emigrated. Ok. I have all the paper work you sent to me by mail and everything looks complete. I will have to talk to Ramsey about his courses and the rules of the school.." "Very good" said my uncle. "now, why don't you have a seat and let me ask you few questions, Ramsey." "Yes sir", I mumbled.

"Ramsey, Do you have any difficulty understanding the English language? Do you prefer to be in a bilingual program?" "I understand it sir, very well indeed. We used to take English every day in My school in Lebanon." I answered. "Excellent. So I will enroll you in the regular classes. Based on your most recent evaluation, you are at grade level, that's good. I suggest you take a literacy class this semester and an easy elective, beside the major courses you HAVE to take, and they are English, Math, social studies and science. We can sign you up in art class as an elective along with literacy, ok?" Mr. Perry asked. "Yes sir, it is ok" I answered. "So far so good, Ramsey. Now, I want to talk to you about discipline and rules. This is a tough city we live in, maybe dramatically different than the city you were raised in, so I want you to stay away from trouble AND troublemakers. I would like you to focus on your studies and work.

There are a lot of good students here whose friendship you would enjoy, I am sure. In all cases, any concerns or hardships you may face, do not hesitate to come and talk to me about them, ok?" Mr. Perry told me. "Ok. Understood, sir" I managed to blurt. I was getting nervous.. What did he mean by tough city? trouble? What kind of trouble? Who are the troublemakers? How would I recognize them? Oh! Wasn't it enough that I already feel like a total stranger, now I have to worry about identifying problems and stay away from them. Minutes later, Mr. Perry offered to escort me to my classroom and introduce me to my homeroom teacher.

My homeroom was on the first floor, located on the North end of the building. Room number 164. The bright lights in the room were so intense and welcoming. I immediately felt at ease with the new space that was to be my "home" for most of the day. Standing next to the blackboard and reading a note, a tall young blond female teacher looked up and managed to smile at the stranger standing at the door. Mr. Perry made the introductions very quickly, delivered me to my teacher Ms. Jenkins and headed back out. My uncle waved goodbye and left. And there I was, alone again, my dejection festering inside. My only solace was the great smiling face looking at me, inviting me in this new world where I can possibly try to fit and fancy about good days to come. Ms. Jenkins seemed to be very nice. She immediately proceeded to explain my schedule to me, pointing out my different classes and their locations. Math in room 205 on the second floor, science in room 323 on the third floor, English in room 165 on the first floor, Literacy in room 209 on the second floor, and my art class will be in room 300 on the third floor...I was overwhelmed with all the details and the information to be absorbed. We would report to homeroom in the morning, right after the bell. We would stay in homeroom for 12 minutes, enough for Ms. Jenkins to take attendance and pass out any papers, lunch and bus tickets. We would then proceed to our next class for A period. I never had to change classes in my old school. Why do we have to do this? Why all the traveling upstairs then downstairs? Why don't we stay in one classroom, and the teachers would come to us?

By the end of C period, right as I was getting frantic and disordered, it was time for lunch. My mother's typical Lebanese lunch allowed me to relax and catch my breath. I had started feeling almost lethargic from the intensity of the confusion and the feeling of being alienated and unfocused. I was sitting in the cafeteria, the noise deafening, the motion endless and my sadness inconsolable. I was looking forward to going home, lock myself in my bedroom and never get out again. I didn't want to have friends, I didn't want to learn, I didn't want to go to school. I could never belong here. This could never be "home". I was in the moping mode, except nobody was willing to listen. I wanted to vent, to scream and cry, the pain inside my head was becoming torrid. As I looked down at my half-way eaten banana, I remembered my best friend Danny, whom I grew up and went to school, and played varsity basket ball with. I had said goodbye to him, the day before we flew to America. We were both deeply silent, saying few words here and there but avoiding eye contact. I had promised to write to him and email him on a daily basis but since we didn't have an internet connection yet at home, I couldn't live up to my promise. I wish I could talk to him. He was the only friend I could trust, the only one I could relate to and identify with. He probably found another teammate by now. Another friend to replace me. I will ask my mother if I could call him, I thought as the bell rang ending lunchtime.

The rest of my school day dragged for another three periods, leaving my puzzled mind in a mixture of confusion and yearning. The yearning, I could explain.

Chapter Four

As I trudged up the gravel path that led to the front of the house, I waved to uncle George who had picked me up from school at 2:30. My day was extremely long. When the dismissal bell finally rang, a humongous sigh of relief escaped my lungs, announcing to my sad heart a short but appreciated period of solace.

My mother was cooking as usual, in her new tiny kitchen where she amazingly managed to fit all her cherished ingredients, recipes, pots and pans. This was her kingdom, her fortress, the platform of her glory, and to see her able to maneuver around the limited space in such lively manner uplifted my spirit for a moment. "Hi honey! tell me how was your day?" she immediately asked me. The look on her face translated her eagerness to know how was my first day. "Horrible!!" I retorted. "Oh, honey! You can't have a severe judgment like this from just one day...Tell me about your teachers, are they nice? Did you meet any new friends? Is the" "Mom, mom, slow down," I interrupted, "I will tell you everything in a little while.. I just feel tired and overwhelmed. Everything is different. I mean, the system is totally new and I have to adapt to it but I feel so alone and dumb. There are a lot of things that I don't understand and terms I have never heard before. I feel like an alien, really mom. I don't think I'm going back tomorrow." I finished. "What are you talking about? What will you father say? You can't just stay home and lament for the rest of the year! Honey, we agreed that this would take time.. Give it time. It is your FIRST day, it's normal to feel alienated and dejected, but it will be fine. Trust me." My mother said as she reached out to give a big hug and God, did I need one! I wanted to cry on her shoulder and tell her how much I missed my old school where Danny, Joe, Naji, Tony and Mahmoud were now. Together. And I was alone here. I wanted to scream and remind her of all my good times spent with my friends in class, all our school plays, our science projects, our summer camps, our school parties. I wanted to tell her how much I wished I would go back to Lebanon and be me again and have my normal quiet life. But I didn't. Instead, I took a deep breath and said "I love you mom".

Dinner was hardly quiet. My father and my sister didn't stop asking me questions about my school. They wanted to know everything: schedule, teachers, cafeteria, classmates... Everything. It was like going through the dire day all over again and made me sense how ghastly it would be to go to school the following day.

Ms. Jenkins greeted all her students like she did the day before. As soon as she took attendance, she passed out our lunch tickets and bus passes. I never had a lunch ticket before. In Lebanon, all students brought home snacks that were consumed during two separate 15 minutes recess periods. Lunch in Lebanon, was the most important meal of the day. It was usually served around 2:00 O'clock which made it easy for students to go have lunch at home with their families. The cafeteria lunch was a new experience to me. One positive outlook of it was bringing students together on one table, exploring new levels of fellowship and possibly friendship. It sure brought Dylan and Cory into my world. My lonely world.

It was my second day of school. Seatings in the cafeteria had been assigned to all students and as soon as I sat in mine, I noticed that two of my homeroom classmates were seated next to me. We looked at each other and, one of them, the tall blond athlete smiled to me in acknowledgment. I smiled back, awkwardly. "Hey, you are in my homeroom. My name is Dylan, what is yours?" The tall one asked. "My name is Ramsey." I managed to answer. I didn't know what to say anymore. The fear of messing up or pronouncing a word the wrong way terrified me. maybe it was better to keep my mouth shut and wait. But what if they thought I was dumb? I looked at the other one. Shorter, darker and considerably chubbier, he was already halfway through his lunch. He stopped chewing for a moment and interjected "my name is Cory. Nice meeting you Ramsey. Do you play basketball?" "I used to." I answered. "USED to?" asked Cory. "Well, yes I used to be in the varsity of my old school." I said. "Oh. Where do you come from? Another state?" inquired Dylan. "no. I come from another country." I confessed. "Wow! I thought I picked up a different accent." replied Dylan, and then continued "Which country is that?" "It is a country in the Middle East region, called Lebanon." I explained. "I have never heard of it." Said Cory, with a noticeable frown on his face. "It is a significantly small country on the Mediterranean sea, far far away from America." I said. "Oh, Ok. Do you like it here?" Dylan surprised me with his question. "I, I am fine...I think I need more time to adjust and..." Cory cut me off by saying "Don't worry, we'll help you out. we'll be buddies." It was probably the most relieving thing I have heard in a long time and it made me feel content. I smiled to my new conquered friends and we spent the rest of our lunchtime telling each other about our lives, hobbies and cultures.

Dylan was an only child. He and his family lived on Pleasant street, two streets away from where we now lived. He was a basketball player by excellence, according to him, and played for the school team. His grades were not excellent, but as far as he was concerned, he was passing and that was enough.

Cory also was a basketball player and on the school team. He came from a family of five: His parents, two sisters and himself. They also lived in the neighborhood but they owned their own beautiful house because

Cory's father was a lawyer and his mother a nurse. Cory's grades were suffering though. He was having a hard time with his majors especially Math. He blamed it on the teachers but in fact, he hardly ever studied nor did any homework. All he was interested in was basketball. All the time. At least, all of us agreed on one thing: We all loved Basketball.

Cory and Dylan were very good to me. They opened the window to a new perspective of the whole immigration experience. I was slowly coming out of my constant melancholy and heading towards an new phase of finding myself and exploring new altitudes of living and possibly happiness. Cory, Dylan and I bonded in a simple spontaneous, uncomplicated way, where we didn't allow our diversities to interfere in the genuine relationship we were building. There is a stranger inside of me, a foreigner who goes astray at times and endure the severity of the bumps along the path. I no longer feel despondent and hopeless. The new acquired friendships gave me a light, a found torch that made me realize that life goes on and that we need to make the best of it. Wherever we are.

Chapter Five

"You should sign up for the February try-outs, Ramsey" Cory blurted out one day after finishing a long one on one match of Basketball. We had been playing for a while, relentless, unstoppable, undisturbed except for the recurrent remarks and praises made by Cory. That is what I most liked about him. His positive attitude and constant encouragement of people make it so easy for everybody around him to like him and appreciate his company. "I don't know, Cory. Do you think I would make it?" I answered him. "Are you kidding? Of course you would. You are the best player I have ever played with, or should I say against?" said Cory with a resonant laugh.

The varsity team of Basketball! I have always loved the game but I wasn't sure about my chances here in the USA. I didn't think I measured up to all the players on the team. The try-outs were not scheduled until February which was barely three weeks away. Not only I still had time to practice but also to train myself mentally for this significant challenge.

For the weeks to follow, I put in order a day plan which allowed me to practice basketball after school during weekdays. Cory and Dylan were there every day. Sometimes, even before even I got there. I learned all the slang language that go with the American Basketball. All the expressions, the tricks and unique moves. I decided to give it all that I have, all my diligence, perseverance and dedication. I surprised myself with being so assiduous and applied. I never missed any homework. I made a vow to myself to be on top of things. At least until I successfully make the varsity Basketball team.

What I knew of coach Radditz was not helping my state of mind. He had been coaching the varsity team for ten years after a retired career in physical education. He had led our middle school Basketball team to a stage of glory and he was adamant to keep its team record as shiny as ever. He was known to be a strict coach and a hard-hitting leader. He only picked the best to play on his team. It took Cory and Dylan weeks of rough training and practicing to get their spots on the team. And once you get your spot, all the hard work launches! Mr. Radditz was religious about practice hours and I knew that. I realized that the only way to achieve my goal, is to acquire Mr. Radditz's acceptance.

"Ramsey, did you mark your calendar?" Dylan asked me one day, right after Math class. "for what?" I answered. "The try-outs man. The date is February 16th at the Gym." Dylan replied. "OKKay", I exhaled. A mixed wave of excitement and anxiety invaded my body. I have to get in. I have to.

A Little Odd

It was a cold rainy day. I had woken up very early, gotten out of bed, put on my clothes and waited. As I waited, I tried to prepare myself mentally and psychologically. I tried to reach the athlete inside of me, the strong person I wanted to be. I almost attained to that state if it wasn't for the constant tapping of the rain drops on my window. Breakfast was scant. I couldn't eat my usual bowl of cocoa puffs. "I would make up for it during lunch", I thought to myself.

I had to endure a long day at school. I wasn't sure I could survive until I heard the release bell and I knew I was so close to face the challenge.

"Start by jogging around for five laps guys and we'll get started soon afterwards", coach Radditz stated to all the new comers, including me. Five boys, two of whom I recognized from common classes, and I were competing for two openings in the varsity team. As I was silently warming up with them around the court, I could spot Dylan and Cory in the front seats of the stadium. I smiled towards them, pretending I am keeping cool and relaxing, trying by all means to hide my strain and rigidity.

Soon after, coach Radditz split us up in two teams of three and announced the beginning of the match. My teammates were extremely skillful. They caught up with my style and we played in perfect harmony against our opponents, which made me wonder about coach Radditz and the difficult task he would have to face in order to pick only two of us. I managed somehow to get my thinking back on the track of the game and pushed myself to focus on dribbling, giving the right passes and mostly shooting. I missed my first two shots. Disappointment rushed to my heart and I could see my chance of making the team dwindling little by little. This could not happen now. I was too close to give up. Not like this. Flashes of my old school and my old team came to me. I remembered times of sweat, joy and praising. I focused on the spirit that got me thus far in this game. I imagined Danny and Mahmoud cheering for me in the audience. It was my happy zone. The ball was in my hand. I was sweating profusely by then, not only from my exhaustion but mostly from my tension. I didn't want to lose my opportunity. I looked around for my teammate to pass the ball.

My eyes locked Cory's and I remembered his encouragement and words of support all along. I smiled at him, realizing at that moment how much I valued his friendship and Dylan's. I thought how odd it is to seek my happy zone from my previous life, when two genuinely fine friends were sitting right by my side in this time of trial. A deep breath ravaged my lungs and in one second, I threw the swinging ball, knowing in my heart it was going in for a three-pointer.

"Alright, It's a wrap kids. Give me two minutes and I'll let you know." coach Radditz declared right after the buzzer.

Cory and Dylan were too excited for me. They thought I played tremendously well. I was too tired to think or even hope.

I looked at coach Radditz who was examining his clipboard and I couldn't read any of his face's signs. I had to wait. Wait.

Two centuries went by. "Okay kids, gather up please." coach Radditz seemed to have reached a decision and was ready to share it with us. I stood there, amongst the other kids, Dylan and Cory in the back. "First, I want to say that you all are well trained kids", coach Radditz started by saying. "But as you know, only two spots are available in the team. I find myself compelled to make a tough decision about this, based on skills, strategy and performance. As I am going to read off the two names, I want to thank the rest and don't forget that there will always be a next time. Ok. The two boys who are joining this varsity team for the new season are: Stan and Ramsey." Coach Radditz finished.

The first reaction anybody could hear came from Cory who screamed his lungs out in cheers. Dylan was too happy to speak and I broke in the most nervous laughter I have ever experienced. This was ecstasy. It was far more than a victory. It was a beautiful window that was opened to me in a world of darkness.

Life was smiling at me. I didn't want to think of Lebanon today. Today, America was pampering me. It was being kind and generous to me and I wanted to enjoy the moment, to freeze the joy and live my dream.

Chapter Six

The weeks that followed my joining of the varsity were delightful and glamorous for me. I didn't mind the long arduous hours of training that I had to attend three times a week. Besides, I was spending most of my afternoons doing what I love most and with my best friends. Life in America had started to look brighter and deep in my heart, I started feeling a strange sense of belonging.

The good thing about the whole matter is that my grades in school did not get affected. My father had been worried about me not being able to catch up in the first place and adjust to the totally different system of learning; so when I joined the varsity team, he got highly skeptical about my capacity of juggling school and basketball. I made it a point to apply myself even harder every day, in order to compromise between the two. So far, I was amazingly doing fine.

My coach was a stern leader. Training with him seemed to be a boot camp more than anything else. Perseverance was his middle name and he did not put up with indolent sluggish players.

One afternoon, as we were leaving the locker room after practice, coach Radditz said: "I guess you all are going to the school dance next Saturday, right?"..I was surprised. I had no idea there was any dance coming up soon. I gave Cory an inquisitive look. "Oh, yes Ramsey. I forgot to tell you. There is a dance for seventh and eight graders next Saturday. It is posted on the classroom bulletin board." said Cory. "Oh. I have never attended one here. Is it nice?" I inquired. "we'll have a good time, Ramsey. You will see. Besides, we know the majority of the students.. What do you think?" Dylan interjected. "I will ask my parents." I finally answered. I wasn't sure I was ready for an event this big. I was ten years old the last time I had attended a school party. Almost three years ago, in Lebanon. I had wanted to go because Nadia, my classmate then, was going. I had worn my new jacket and some of my dad's perfume, hoping to impress the most beautiful girl in my school. Nadia was a very popular girl and almost every body in school wanted to be her friend or sit next to her. And as attractive as she was, she also was totally oblivious about it. A very kind, down-to-earth and humble girl who exuded joy and beauty. I remembered dancing next to her, feeling the thrill of being in her entourage and enjoying the first kick of what is called Love. I didn't want that night to end, but when it did, I had realized that Nadia was definitely not interested in me or anybody else for that matter.

Here I am, three years later, thousands of miles away, about to attend my first party in America. Excitement engulfed my heart. I gasped for air, for joy.

The perfectly decorated gym used for the party was merely unrecognizable. The high-tech sound and music system installed was impressive. But what caught my attention the most were the lightings. Evenly circulated around the area used for the dance floor, the color-changing bulbs added a fascinating aura of celebration, festivity and somewhat joy. Many students had arrived before us and I could recognize most of them. Cory and Dylan had no problem mingling with our fellow students. They had so much to tell about the varsity team, coach Radditz and the training itself. Basketball was unquestionably the most important spot of our lives but tonight, I was ready for a break. Walking amongst my schoolmates was starting to become a little boring when I spotted her at the end of the cheer leaders tables, sitting by herself, talking on a cell phone. I recognized her from the cheer leaders club. Tonight, she seemed different, more relaxed and in different clothes. She wore her long chestnut hair down for the first time and boy! it was gorgeous. I looked around, checking if anybody was watching the scene and to my relief, everybody was busy with their own scenarios. Even Cory and Dylan were out of sight. I worked up my dim courage and convinced myself that this was my chance to get to know her better. Even the thought of her mocking my accent did not interfere with my plan. Well, usually it did. But not tonight. No.

As I approached her, her conversation on the phone seemed to be reaching an end. "Ok Lindsay, I'll call you tomorrow." I couldn't help hear. "bye". The phone was off and I stood there, behind her seat, still hesitating. All of a sudden, she turned around and looked at me with big interrogative eyes. "Hi" I finally managed to utter. "Hi", she answered, smiling. "I don't know if you recall me, I am the new drafted player on the Basketball varsity team. I have seen you with the cheer leaders." I started. "Oh. yes, Ramsey, right? I didn't recognize you in your regular clothes. We are used to seeing you guys, in your shorts and jerseys. Sorry!" she apologized. "No problem. May I know your name?" I asked while beginning to relax. "I am Ashley, nice to meet you

Ramsey." She said. "Thank you, same here. Are you having fun?" I inquired. "It's ok. My friends couldn't come tonight. I am a little disappointed but it's alright. Are you?" She shot back. "I just got here ten minutes ago. Cory and Dylan are here too. You know them, right?" I said.

"I think so. You have a nice accent." She remarked. Oh! God! I thought. There we go with the accent thing. I had hoped to be able to erase it somehow but I guess it is built in my vocal cords leading me to believe it will remain there forever. "Well, Thank you. Would you like me to get you a drink?" I asked. "Sure, I will have a diet coke please." She replied. "I will be right back" I said and headed to the refreshment booth to get two diet cokes. I wondered on my way whether she would be still there when I came back and I almost burst out laughing. Evidently, she was waiting for me, thanked me for the drink and proceeded to sip it immediately. "So, do you like Basketball, Ramsey?" she asked. "I have always liked it. It is my passion. I hope to be a NBA player one day." I elaborated.

"Wow, That's awesome. Great!" She exclaimed. "Do you enjoy cheer leading?" I tried to keep the conversation going. "I do and I don't. I have been doing this for two years and it is basically the same routine. I want a new hobby!" She answered. "What else do you like?" I asked. "I like reading and acting. I am considering joining the Drama club. What do you think, Ramsey. Do I have the face of an actress?" she laughingly asked.

"Oh yes, yes. You are very pretty." I couldn't believe I said that. I could feel the rush of blushing raging my face and thank God it was rather dark in there, so she could not see my embarrassment. Amazingly enough, she was very candid about it and took it graciously. "Thank you". As I was trying to come up with something new to say, the loud music interrupted me and clapping followed. Groups of students flowed in to the dance floor and started dancing to the beat. I looked at Ashley's face which lit up in the glowing lights and her smile lit up my heart. "Would you like to dance?" I offered. She didn't even have to answer with words. She immediately stood up and held my hand to lead the way. My heart was racing harder than the beating music. I resorted to watch others in order to get a hang of how to dance. Ashley didn't need to follow no leader. She knew how to dance. She knew how to dance well. Her vigorous body tamed the music and I was in awe. I was in heaven. I shockingly managed to somewhat echo her beat of steps and I perfectly fit in the crowd. She kept smiling at me, forcing my heart to take long dangerous leaps of joy and ecstasy.

We danced and danced until we couldn't feel our feet. Even notorious Ashley complained by 11 O'clock. We stopped and sat at the nearest table, trying to catch our breaths. This is when I decided to act on my impulse and hit her with the most courageous question I had to come up with in my life. "Can I have your phone number

Ashley?" She took a long sip from her cold diet coke, swallowed and looked at me. "I like you too Ramsey." She bent forward, grabbed my pen from my shirt and jotted her phone number on her napkin then stood up and said "I'm sorry but my mother should be waiting for me outside. It's eleven. Time to go." I escorted her all the way to the door where she turned one last time and said in a very soft voice "I enjoyed your company tonight. I am waiting for your call. Goodnight" "Goodnight" I said sadly.

When I turned around to head back, I found Cory and Dylan standing there, smiling, waiting. I knew I had a lot of explaining and telling to do!

Chapter Seven

The weeks that followed the party were extremely busy. I got swept with a rush of new feelings and the traditions and habits of the American culture when it came to dating. All the memories of the shy me and the elusive Nadia and all the dreams and fantasies that accompanied that period went dwindling in the very back of my head. I was facing a tremendously different era of romancing, dating and having a girlfriend. Back in Lebanon, you couldn't date or think of having a girlfriend/boyfriend before college. The cultural barriers were thick and high and rules were scarcely bent. So when I first announced to my parents that my "girlfriend" was coming over to my house one Friday afternoon, their faces went white with surprise and awkwardness. And of course, I had to hear the long and classic speech of caution, prudence and wisdom for hours. "It's no big deal, mom. She is just coming over to study and hang out with all of us." I pleaded. "ok, ok. But listen to your daddy." My mother uncomfortably answered.

My relationship with Ashley, on the other hand, was undoubtedly going way better than I ever expected. Being the most self-confident down-to-earth girl I have ever met, she had no problem understanding my background and absorbing the roughness of my edges and mostly my hesitance. She made an extra effort every time to explain miscellaneous bits and pieces to me and I found myself completely at ease with her and eventually with myself.

On Saturdays, I would meet her at her house and we would walk together to the bus station where we took the bus to the mall. There we would walk around and then catch an early afternoon showing of the current movie. It was great, except for the fact that I couldn't hang out with my best friends as often as I used to but they understood and we still saw each other in classes. So when Ashley came over to my house, she won my parents hearts over in a flash and she felt so comfortable around them almost immediately. All reservations my mother and father had about us vanished immediately.

They loved her just the same as I did her. My mother later developed the habit of inviting her every Friday over for dinner and that brought happiness to almost all of us. Even my sister Raya got to be very fond of Ashley, attempting to relate to her and identify with her as a teenager in any beneficial way possible.

The best part of it all, is that we stayed diligent and serious about our respective involvement with the Varsity Basketball team. Nothing had prepared me to what was stored for me next in the vast world of my passionate game.

A Little Odd

The news of the Basketball summer camp on the island of Martha's Vineyard dashed into my settled life like a hurricane that enticed my fantasies day and night. The event was coach Radditz's idea in concept and execution. He had been mentioning it to all of his players for a considerable time. His major aspiration is to give us a chance to try out for the National Youth Basketball league. The league drafts new players for its national team every year from all over the United States and inducts them in its one and only national Varsity team which would represent the whole country in National tournaments and possibly the Olympics. Basically, it was every Basketball player's dream and fantasy and for me to have the opportunity to have a shot at it is tremendously exciting.

"Dad, it is only six weeks!" I exclaimed to my father, one night over dinner as I attempted to explain my wish. "Six weeks?? Who will take care of you. You have never been away from home. Ever!" replied my father with anguish. "But dad, this is a golden opportunity for all of us. It is a wonderful experience and a precious chance for me to be one of the best. Please dad!" I pleaded again. "But where will you stay? It is six weeks, not just overnight Ramsey" My father inquired. "The school will provide housing for the players and coaches and it is convenient because it is about a 20 minutes walk to the main gym where we would be practicing." I answered. "Why do you have to go to that island to practice. You are practicing here in the school gym, right?" my father asked anxiously. "Well, the National Youth Basketball is touring the whole country and its next stop will be Martha's Vineyard in the attempt to get the Cape Cod area involved more effectively this year. This is why coach Radditz organized this camp. So what do you think Dad?" I thoroughly laid out the matter to my father. "I am a little concerned about you staying away from home but I promise you I will think about it." said my father.

A wave of relief invaded my heart and the glow of hope was vivid in my eyes.

Ashley was definitely thrilled for me and since she would be there too with all the other cheer leaders, especially to cheer us up during the friendly games with the local teams, this camp was seeming to be an exquisite event to all of us. Cory's and Dylan's parents did not object at all and gave their respective sons their full consent. For my father, who was struggling with the idea of his thirteen year old son to be away for that long a time, eventually conceded and agreed especially after long talks and pleas from my mother. I had begged her for days and days, promising her to do all chores and be at the top of my class and, mostly, stay away from trouble.

I have yet to embark on an intricate episode of my life that would sharply define and mold my character.

Chapter Eight

The rest of the year dragged at a snail's pace, leaving me wondering about Martha's Vineyard and the upcoming experience. I had promised my father to excel at my studies, so I applied myself every night, giving my best at all subjects. I still didn't and couldn't miss any practice session but whatever I was doing, my dream of becoming a national basketball player never abandoned my thoughts.

My parents were fairly getting used to the idea of sending me away for a relatively long period of time. It was a gradual plodding phase of anticipation and concern. All I could do during that period is give my best and prove that I could be responsible and deliver my promises. Ashley was always there to give me a boost whenever I felt anxious and impatient. The fact that she was going to the island as well made the whole experience more appealing and interesting. I loved her so much and I needed her to be there for me and with me as I may become a national basketball player.

Dylan and Cory had a good chance too. They were both excellent players and the best teammates. I could not fathom the fact that, one day, we might very well compete for the same spot. It was our dream, yet we never thought it we would stand to fight against each other, as opponents. We never talked about it. It seemed like we all had our own reasoning about the matter but not courageous enough to face our feelings and discuss it openly. They probably thought that, (just like I did), they would cross that bridge when they got to it. Which made perfect sense. It was too early to make assumptions and distress our special friendship ahead of time.

Summer finally came! On June 23rd that year, we had an early release because it was the last day of school. Cory, Dylan, Ashley and I walked back to school on a very sunny warm day, relieved and ecstatic. It was over! The long somewhat difficult year was at last over and that meant it was almost time to head to Martha's Vineyard for the Basketball camp. Mr. Radditz had told us the week before, that we would leave on July6th and return on August 17th. All of us. Winners and losers.

I spent the whole week, working out, meeting at the gym every day with the rest of the team, packing, and anticipating every minute of the six weeks we would spend there. My parents tried their best not to display their anxiety but supported me and my dream all the way till the end.

The bus left from the school's parking lot at eight Am on July 6th, going towards Woodshole harbor, hoping to make it for the 9:30 ferry to the island of Martha's Vineyard.

The boat ride was smooth and slow, unlike my emotions and thoughts. For most of the ride, Ashley sat next to me on the deck, quiet and calm. Each one of our school team was absorbed in his own thoughts and feelings. Even Coach Raddtiz, spent the whole trip staring at the water wrapping around the ship crossing the ocean..

We settled down in the big dormitory of the Martha's vineyard High school. The island was hosting the National youth Basketball league for the first time and teams from four major cities of Cape Cod were on the island to compete for a spot on the national team.

The concentrated training we had to endure every day did not give any of us the chance to go sightseeing on the beautiful island except for very few times. Our coach reserved a tour for us, one Sunday morning (total surprise for us!) and showed us around. From Oak Bluffs to Edgartown then to Gay Head, the most attractive nature I had ever seen on earth! Along the Beach coast of Martha's Vineyard sprawled along the most exquisite ocean of silky silvery water embracing long stretches of golden powdery sand. After a little stroll on the native American Moshup Trail, we had to go back to Edgartown, where the High school was located. What I liked the most was walking from the High school to the main gym in the community center nearby. The outlandish green trees hugging both sides of the streets, dancing Tango with the humming wind, inviting gorgeous birds to enjoy this celebration of God's most stunning creations, made this twenty minutes walk a healing break away from our hectic schedule. I loved it. The silent rocky brook that find its passage through the thick boughs of virgin trees reminded me of the necessity of hope in the midst of a trying and tough time.

And I had hope.

Chapter Nine

The most engaging time of every day was meeting Ashley for dinner in the big High school cafeteria and discuss the different stories and events of the day. She was as thrilled about the experience as I was, If not more. It made it easier for me to juggle my two identities and adapt to this new phase. After calling our respective parents, we would sit and watch Television with all the other players, coaches, and cheer leaders. The general talk was about my good chance to be drafted, according to all who saw me on the court. Not only I was gaining coach Radditz's praise but also my fellow players' and mostly my own. I had done as advised by all my peers. I had worked diligently towards this moment and I wanted it more than anything in the world. I believed in myself and worked up all my energy and self-confidence along with my hard work to fulfill my longed for dream. I often thought, that had I been still living in Lebanon, this opportunity would have never presented itself to me.. Or would it? This ought to be the land of dreams, like every body says. The days of longing for my past life and my unforgettable roots had begun to dwindle somewhere deep in my mind.

"I have great faith in you, Rams" Ashley said one evening, two days before the big day. "Oh Ashley! This means so much to me. I am starting to get a little nervous." I answered. "Oh stop being silly. You know you are good." Ashley replied. "I know that there are other excellent players as well." I said with a laugh. "But you will be better" finished Ashley, winking.

The following two days were chaotic and frantic, not only physically but also emotionally and psychologically. The counting down was getting to the zero level and my anticipation way above 1000!

The last night, every body turned in early in the hope to enjoy a good long night sleep, in preparation for a successful and eventful day. The night was stretched and dire. I had such trouble attempting to rest and relax. But I had to. I had to be at my best the next day. For me. For Ashley. For all those who believed in me. By the crack of dawn, my excitement had gotten the best of me and I woke to a relatively calm atmosphere, where you could hear unhurried and dawdling action in the background, as players, coaches, assistants and cheerleaders were bracing themselves for a remarkable day ahead.

By the time I took my shower and got dressed, most of the players had headed to the center. I was one of the few who lingered behind.

I looked in the mirror and all I could see were eyes glowing with excitement and hope. I started combing my thick dark hair as memories of a whole year took a leap to my mind. My difficult adjustment, the livid workouts, the new perfected strategies on the court.. It was finally here. The big day.

"Be there at 10:00, guys. Don't be late" coach Radditz had warned us the night before and then he leaned towards me and added

"You have a good chance Ramsey. I am counting on you, buddy." I beamed at the thought and the tremendous trust he planted on my shoulders. It almost felt like a burden now that I was extremely nervous, but one that I had promised myself to carry well and beautifully.

On this particularly hot and humid day on Martha's Vineyard, tourists from all over the nation were dashing through the streets.

They, like most people, were curious about this quaint island located on the dazzling Atlantic. It attracted all types of interested people who enjoyed unforgettably stunning natural sights and amazing beaches. Especially hikers who were everywhere exploring all corners of the island from Katama to Gay head to Tisbury and East chop.

I gathered all my needed items in my bag, threw it on my shoulder and headed towards the community center. I embarked on my journey, mulling in my head all the exhilarating things that will happen to me, all the glory, the fame, the success. I usually walked on the barren straightforward road that cut through the town and led to the center but I looked at my watch and realized that I had ten extra minutes, so I decided to adopt the inner wooded path by the brook that dug through the other end of the forest and that led to the center from the back road. I thought that it would give me a chance to relax and loosen up in order to display a better performance. So I did. The other side of the road was mysteriously simple and extravagant at the same time. The raw nature that welcomed me like a giant's embrace soothed my anxiety and pushed me farther into the woods. I thought of Ashley, who is probably wondering what I was still doing and how much she would love to walk on this trail with me and...

"Help! Help! Help!" a cry of pain suddenly shattered my fantasy and I found myself in front of an older man in hiking attire, lying on the ground, his bleeding foot trapped amidst a group of conspiring heavy rocks.

"Oh! Sir, what happened!!?" I shakily asked the wounded man. "I was attempting to cross the river to the other side, but I slipped and got stuck. Is there any way you could help me, young man?" pleaded the stranger with a chuckle. I deliberately started trying to move any of the stubborn rocks, in vain. I looked at the man's foot closely. It was bleeding profusely. "What do I do?" I thought. I eyed the moaning man. He was sweaty, pale and frightened. His injuries were serious and beyond my limited abilities. I looked at my watch. Oh God! I had to walk 20 minutes to reach the center, yet the high school was only five minutes away. But what about my dream?

the league? What do I do? I was fighting time, my torn self and my adolescent values to keep a cherished dream and the precious life of a person. I knew I didn't have time to go to the center first. The helpless man in front of me didn't have enough time. He was getting worse by the second. I had to make a decision fast. Very fast.

Tormented by a sea of conflicting ideas, I closed my eyes and sifted through my sinking heart. All my life came to a stop at this second. And it didn't matter who I was anymore. This was neither about my culture, nor about my new found home. It was about ethics and doing the right thing even if it meant jeopardizing my goals and my aspirations. This moment was defining who I was and who I was supposed to be.

I grimly acknowledged what I had to do. In one gigantic moment, I shifted gear, turned my back to my almost lost dream and headed back to the high school to seek adequate help. The high school was five minutes away. Disappointment was five minutes away.

It was awkward, almost absurd, reassuring the pained man behind. I desperately needed reassurance myself.

The walk back to the high school was excruciating. I was dragging numb feet and carrying a heavy heart. I tried to go faster but my energy was failing. My disappointment was stinging my eyes and burning my throat. Finally, I reached the deserted High school. Another reminder of my sadness. I shouldn't be here. I shouldn't be here. In the lobby, The janitor was still mopping the floor. I looked at his surprised face but didn't say anything. My sweaty palms reached for the main phone and dialed 911. "A man is seriously injured near the Tisbury brook. His foot is deeply bruised." I uttered to the dispatcher. And so is my heart, I craved to say but refrained.

Upon her overpowering request, I somberly agreed to await the paramedics close to the High school, as they didn't know the exact location of the suffering man.

I crashed on the front steps of the school, put my head down and surrendered to my misery. The road ahead of me was wide open, yet I was trapped in my own space, my conscience. How could this have happened to me? Why me?

It was 10:25 when the squealing ambulance dove into my silent desolation. Distraught yet eager to help, I quickly assimilated with the professional paramedics and led the way to where the wounded man lay in pain. We apparently got there in time. He had started to dehydrate and become listless, almost incoherent in the horrendous heat. After delicate and effective attempts to move the rocks without inflicting more extensive damage, the rescuers lifted the injured man on a gurney and transported him to the ambulance.

It was 10:55 by then and the overwhelming sense of loss fell over my heart and I sat there, where a man's life was spared and a boy's dream buried. I had missed it. The golden chance to be what I wanted to be was gone. My journey had ended there, by the Tisbury brook, unexpectedly, abruptly.

I didn't want to wonder what was happening at the other side of the fence. I didn't want to know. I didn't.

I still do not recall how and why I headed to the center anyway. My guess is pure despair and the need for the woe to be materialized.

I arrived at the center's gym around 11:30, embraced by the cheers as loud as my concealed sobs. The gym was expectedly jammed. Everybody in there was applauding for Cory. My best friend Cory was drafted. Jealousy electrified my body but oddly enough I was happy for him as well. He robbed me of my dream but he also was my best friend and my teammate.

There he stood, facing the cheering crowd, his eyes squirting pride, his heart singing victory. He was the one. He had it all. I was nobody. I had nothing. Nothing.

In coach Radditz's office that evening, I held Ashley's warm hand and cried my heart out as I recounted my brush with destiny that morning. They both looked at me in awe, attentive and bewildered. The Golden cup on an upper shelf in that office reminded me of my voracious defeat.

Chapter Ten

The weeks following the event were completely agonizing. I locked myself in my tiny room, alienating myself from the rest of the world, including my worried family. I didn't want to know or hear anything. Even Ashley, who constantly tried to connect with me and cheer me up, didn't succeed. The only reality I was dealing with was my devastation and my despair. I was grieving a stillborn dream, a goal never reached. All I breathed was injustice. I didn't want to be the hero, the valiant. I wanted to be the famous basketball player. My tears didn't help though. I was getting to a point where I started disliking this whining person inside of me who is excelling at playing the role of a victim. That person was not the true me.

"Honey, you have to forget about that already. You will have other chances in the future, I am sure" pleaded my mother day after day. "Yeah, right. That's it for me and basketball" I replied.

I didn't see Cory anymore. He was extremely busy with the new commitment he had with the National league. I remember seeing him after the big day and awkwardly congratulating him. He was so humble, just like I had always known him to be. He probably had sensed my discomfort and said "Hey, you will have your shot one day too, Ramsey. You too, are a great player". I couldn't but smile. But that moment was gone now and he was in different league, preparing one of the busiest season this League will have. Training in different cities and entering in many tournaments locally and overseas.

The thought of going back to school was making me ill at ease. Ashley remarkably convinced me that it would be ok to start over again, a new year and set a new goal. I wanted to tell her I may not have another chance but didn't want to burst her bubble and disappoint her.

Back to school! Again! This year, I was feeling strange in a complete different way. I was a stranger towards myself.

We went back the Tuesday after Labor day as usual. The same routine went on for the first part of the day and by early afternoon, we headed towards the gym. It was the last period of the day and it was kind of convenient for us, since we didn't have to worry about going back to the classroom afterwards.

After changing in the lockers room, we proceeded to going to the basketball court, where we usually met. My classmates, most of whom I knew from last year, were noticeably glancing at me once in a while. I knew they were wondering. I took a deep breath and entered the gym. A big wave of applause and cheers greeted me from all four corners of the gym that took me totally by surprise. Mr. Radditz was also there clapping and smiling in my direction. I had no idea what was going on. I wanted to say "I am sorry. I think you made a mistake. I was NOT drafted. Cory was. You are mistaken." But the whole atmosphere was numbing. When all the clapping settled down, coach Radditz went on to say: "Hello everyone and congratulations Ramsey! Congratulations on being a hero and someone this school and I personally are immensely proud of! What you did on the day of the drafting was extremely honorable and more important than any medal or prize." More clapping and cheering followed and elation started its narrow way to my heart. This genuine thought made me realize how blessed I was to be recognized and thanked. "Mr. Peterson (the man I helped on the island) sent you a nice thank you card and wishes you well Ramsey. He is very grateful" Mr. Radditz continued. I finally smiled and accepted the card and thanked everybody for being so thoughtful, kind and compassionate.

The walk back home was not like any I had before. I knew this would be a new beginning for me. The whole sky could not contain my glee.

Chapter Eleven

Destiny played a crucial role that unforgettable day. It had placed me on that man's path, for an obvious reason. It may have seemed to be a malevolent test. In one instant, I could have gone my way, totally oblivious to Ethics' call. But I didn't. Instead, I put a patch on my selfishness and opted to be brave in my own way. Yes, the stakes were high but glory and fame were such a cheap price for a human life.

I finally came to terms with my loss and the ugly reality of failure. I still have a lot to contend with but whenever a shock of doubt tingles my spirit and regret stands imminent at my door, I resort to the card that Mr. Peterson sent me after his full recovery. His kind expression of admiration and gratefulness refills my heart with confidence and pride.

I don't have a golden cup sitting on my bureau. I don't have a glossy medal mounted on my room's wall. I don't have a championship ring to brag about. It is all lost.

Mr. Peterson's life is my one and only trophy.

In the midst of all that was coming my way, I stop sometimes and wonder about all the new challenges I had to take on, all the cultural differences and the effort to adjust and blend in. I have learned many things along the road, mostly that human nature prevails, wherever you are placed on Earth.

I still feel a little odd in many ways but I know, deep in my heart, that I still can be the true ME and call America, HOME.

About the Author

Marlene Mansour Sabeh is a native of Lebanon. She moved to America in 1995, joining her husband, a longtime resident of Fall River, Massachusetts. She was always passionate about writing, especially writing for youngsters. Along with a degree in Computer Sciences, she earned a diploma in writing for Children's magazines from the institute of children's literature in Connecticut.

This is her first juvenile fiction, which depicts the struggle of an immigrant teenager and his painful journey towards finding his new identity. Since the story is based on a personal experience, "A little odd" sheds a new light on every immigrant's fears and drawbacks from a teenager's perspective.

Marlene Mansour Sabeh targeted young readers since she had the chance to work with middle schools students for four years. She currently holds the position of student coordinator in New Bedford High School, New Bedford, Massachusetts.

With her husband and two children, Marlene Mansour Sabeh divides her time between Fall River and the island of Martha's Vineyard.

Printed in the United States
56864LVS00001B/43-63